THE
GINGERBREAD
BOY

Clarion Books
a Houghton Mifflin Company imprint
215 Park Avenue South, New York, NY 10003
Copyright © 1975 by Paul Galdone
For information about permission to reproduce
selections from this book, write to Permissions,
Houghton Mifflin Company, 215 Park Avenue South, New York, NY 10003
Manufactured in China

Library of Congress Cataloging in Publication Data

Galdone, Paul.
  The gingerbread boy.

  SUMMARY: The Gingerbread Boy eludes the hungry grasp
of everyone he meets until he happens upon a fox more
clever than he.
  [1. Folklore.   2. Fairy tales]   I. Title.
PZ8.1.G15Gi   [398.2]   [E]   74-11461
ISBN 0-395-28799-5   Paperback ISBN 0-89919-163-0

SCP   60 59 58 57 56 55 54 53
4500404661

THE GINGER-BREAD BOY

PAUL GALDONE

Clarion Books
New York

OTHER CLARION BOOKS BY PAUL GALDONE

Once upon a time
there lived a little old woman
and a little old man.
They had no boys or girls
of their own, so they lived
all by themselves
in a little old house.

One day the little old woman
was baking gingerbread.
"I will make a little
Gingerbread Boy," she said.

So she rolled the dough out flat
and cut it in the shape of a little boy.
She made him two good-sized feet.

Then she gave him eyes and a mouth
of raisins and currants,
and stuck on a cinnamon drop for a nose.

She put a row of raisins down the front
of his jacket for buttons.

"There!" she said. "Now we'll have a little Gingerbread Boy of our own."

She put him in the pan, popped him into the oven, and closed the door.

8

Then she went about her work,
sweeping and cleaning, cleaning and sweeping,
and she forgot all about the little Gingerbread Boy.

Meanwhile he baked brown all over and got very hot.

"Oh my!" said the little old woman
at last, sniffing the air.
"The Gingerbread Boy is burning!"

She ran to the oven and opened the door.
Up jumped the Gingerbread Boy.
He hopped down onto the floor,
ran across the kitchen,
out of the door,
across the garden,
through the gate,
and down the road as fast as
his gingerbread legs could carry him.

The little old woman and the little old man ran after him, shouting:
"Stop! Stop, little Gingerbread Boy!"

The Gingerbread Boy looked back and laughed and called out:

"Run! Run! Run!
Catch me if you can!
You can't catch me!
I'm the Gingerbread Boy,
I am! I am!"

And they couldn't catch him.

So the Gingerbread Boy ran on and on.
Soon he came to a cow.
"Um! um!" sniffed the cow. "You smell good!
Stop, little Gingerbread Boy! I would like to eat you."

But the little Gingerbread Boy laughed and said:

"I've run away from a little old woman,
I've run away from a little old man,
And I can run away from you, I can."

So the cow ran after him. But she couldn't catch him.

16

The little Gingerbread Boy ran on and on.
Soon he came to a horse.
"Please stop, little Gingerbread Boy,"
said the horse.
"You look very good to eat."

But the little Gingerbread Boy called out:

"I've run away from a little old woman,
I've run away from a little old man,
I've run away from a cow,
And I can run away from you, I can."

So the horse ran after him. But he couldn't catch him.

By and by the Little Gingerbread Boy came to a barn
where some men were threshing wheat.
The threshers saw the little Gingerbread Boy and called:
"Do not run so fast, little Gingerbread Boy.
Gingerbread boys are made to eat."

But the little Gingerbread Boy ran faster and faster
and shouted:

"I've run away from a little old woman,
  I've run away from a little old man,
  I've run away from a cow,
  I've run away from a horse,
  And I can run away from you,
  I can, I can!"

So the threshers ran after him. But they couldn't catch him.

The little Gingerbread Boy ran faster than ever.
Soon he came to a field full of mowers.
When the mowers saw how fine he looked, they called:
"Wait a bit! Wait a bit, little Gingerbread Boy!
Gingerbread boys are made to eat."

But the Gingerbread Boy laughed harder than ever
and ran on like the wind. "Oh, ho! Oh, ho!" he cried:

"I've run away from a little old woman,
I've run away from a little old man,
I've run away from a cow,
I've run away from a horse,
I've run away from a barn full of threshers,
And I can run away from you,
I can, I can!"

So the mowers ran after him.

But they couldn't catch him.

By this time the little Gingerbread Boy was very proud
of himself. He strutted, he danced, he pranced!
He thought no one on earth could catch him.

Then he saw a fox coming across the field.
The fox looked at him and began to run.

But the little Gingerbread Boy ran faster still, and shouted:

"Run! Run! Run!
Catch me if you can!
You can't catch me!
I'm the Gingerbread Boy,
I am! I am!
I've run away from a little old woman,
I've run away from a little old man,
I've run away from a cow,
I've run away from a horse,
I've run away from a barn full of threshers,
I've run away from a field full of mowers,
And I can run away from you,
I can! I can!"

"Why," said the fox politely,
"I wouldn't catch you if I could."

Just then the little Gingerbread Boy came to a wide river.
He dared not jump into the water, for he would
crumble to pieces if he did. He looked behind him.
The cow, the horse, and all the people were still
following and getting closer. He had to cross the
river, or they would catch him.

The fox saw this and said,
"Jump on my tail and I will take you across."
So the little Gingerbread Boy jumped onto the fox's tail
and the fox jumped into the river.

When they were out in the river, the fox said:

29

"Little Gingerbread Boy,
I think you had better get
on my back or you may fall off!"
So the little Gingerbread Boy jumped on the fox's back.

After swimming a little farther, the fox said:

"The water is deep.
You may get wet where you are.
Jump up on my shoulder."

So the little Gingerbread Boy jumped up on the fox's shoulder.

When they were near the
other side of the river,
the fox cried out suddenly:
"The water grows deeper still.
Jump up on my nose!
Jump up on my nose!"

So the little Gingerbread Boy jumped up on the fox's nose.

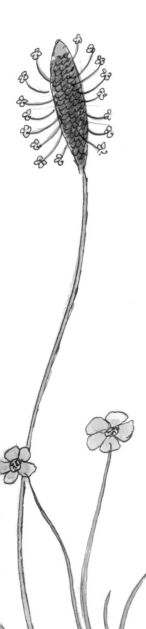

The fox sprang ashore and threw back his head.
Snip—half the Gingerbread Boy was gone.
Snip, *Snap*—he was three-quarters gone.

Snip, *Snap*, *Snip*,
at last and at last
he went the way of
every single gingerbread boy
that ever came
out of an oven....

He was all gone!

So the little old woman and the little old man,
and the cow and the horse,
and the threshers and the mowers,
all went home again...

39

...while the fox had a good long nap.

40